T0128644

SPACE WALKER

By
Mr. Babak Naderi
Fiction

Note for Librarians: a cataloguing record for this book that includes Dewey Decimal Classification and US Library of Congress numbers is available from the Library and Archives of Canada. The complete cataloguing record can be obtained from their online database at:
www.collectionscanada.ca/amicus/index-e.html
Printed in Victoria, BC, Canada

Order this book online at www.trafford.com
or email orders@trafford.com

Most Trafford titles are also available at major online book retailers.

 **www.trafford.com**

North America & international
toll-free: 844 688 6899 (USA & Canada)
fax: 812 355 4082

Printed on paper with minimum 30% recycled fibre. Trafford's print shop runs on "green energy" from solar, wind and other environmentally-friendly power sources.

Offices in Canada, USA, Ireland and UK
This book was published *on-demand* in cooperation with Trafford Publishing. On-demand publishing is a unique process and service of making a book available for retail sale to the public taking advantage of on-demand manufacturing and Internet marketing. On-demand publishing includes promotions, retail sales, manufacturing, order fulfilment, accounting and collecting royalties on behalf of the author.

Book sales for North America and international:
Trafford Publishing, 6E–2333 Government St.,
Victoria, BC v8t 4p4 CANADA
phone 250 383 6864 (toll-free 1 888 232 4444)
fax 250 383 6804; email to orders@trafford.com

Book sales in Europe:
Trafford Publishing (uk) Limited, 9 Park End Street, 2nd Floor
Oxford, UK ox1 1hh UNITED KINGDOM
phone 44 (0)1865 722 113 (local rate 0845 230 9601)
facsimile 44 (0)1865 722 868; info.uk@trafford.com

Order online at: trafford.com/07-0673

10 9 8 7 6 5 4 3 2 1

Our mission is to efficiently provide the world's finest, most comprehensive book publishing service, enabling every author to experience success. To find out how to publish your book, your way, and have it available worldwide, visit us online at www.trafford.com

Because of the dynamic nature of the Internet, any web addresses or links contained in this book may have changed since publication and may no longer be valid. The views expressed in this work are solely those of the author and do not necessarily reflect the views of the publisher, and the publisher hereby disclaims any responsibility for them.

Any people depicted in stock imagery provided by Getty Images are models, and such images are being used for illustrative purposes only.
Certain stock imagery © Getty Images.

ISBN: 978-1-4251-2272-0 (sc)

ISBN: 978-1-4669-7433-3 (e)

Print information available on the last page.

Trafford rev. 02/11/2021

"In Memory of Mr. Joseph Brennan."

"Which came first the number or the noise?" I asked the old man. He said "Twelve is your magic number." Why don't I stop and think about it, I do not know even to this day.

Before I can tell you, the reader, how the old man died that day; I must tell you how we got here, on earth. It is a state of bliss, harmony, and absolute beauty; it is a perfect planet far, far away beyond the known Sun, beyond the known Milkyway Galaxy, beyond the well known black hole in the universe. It is pure euphoria, eventhough there is no Sun shining down on it, the blue planet is shining on its own every day. It is mostly made out of pure matter. There is also enough oxygen in the air to last a billion life times over and over again.

There it is, the most famous blue planet on the modern man's lips. That is where we all come from. It pops out and spins away from the black hole like a blown up helium balloon at a birthday party. The blue planet defies all the gravitational forces of the black hole. It is suspended in the universe, just above the entrance into the black hole and it is protected by a ring of intense fire. This is the planet on which, you never age or die, there will be no wrinkles on your face. There is an abundance of food and there is no waste or garbage to worry about. Everything is used and absorbed to its potential.

There is a flow of energy through out the planet, that enables everyone to never get tired and fatigued. It is an absolute state of ecstacy. It is a place of satisfaction and every pleasure known to mankind. This is a place where there are no tragedies and no one loses their mind and goes crazy, and you are never embarrassed nor rejected.

There is no conflict nor disputes, and you can appear or disappear whenever and wherever you want.

The arc of fire around the blue planet is brighter and stronger than the known Sun. The blue planet's outer limit orbits as an enormous ring of fire. It twists and turns around the planet, and it twirls around its own circumference in all directions. Its sunlike shine is much more intense and brighter than the known Sun. Its burning heat will never die out. This arc of light has no effect on the planet's brightness, its primary function is to protect the blue planet from outer space's unknown stars and comets crashing towards the planet. The ring of fire's gravitational and centripetal forces help the planet to be at the front and center of the black hole, suspended in utter darkness. Unlike Kepler's and Newton's laws of orbital planets and unlike elliptical orbits, such as the Sun and the solar system, this ring of fire is circular. It does not have a closest point periapsis nor the farthest point apoapsis in its orbital movement. And its core is made of 99 percent pure hydrogen and that is why it is so powerful.

On the other hand, Helios is an everlasting ball of fire. It is the center of the solar system. Its core is made of mostly hydrogen and partly made of helium. It takes fifteen minutes to lose your eye sight staring straight into the Sun. People have worshiped the Sun for thousands and thousands of years, believing that it is the most powerful being in the universe. At the crack of dawn the rooster crows, and at high noon its highest point glows. It is dying inside ever so slowly and the globe is getting warmer and warmer with it. It is a candle of hope in the midst of uncertainty. Its waves of light break through the clouds, and its sunspots mole its face. During solar eclipses, people thought of the devil killing the Sun and so they killed the evil on earth at the same time. The Sun changes its magnetic field every eleven years or so and that is also how it reaches out into the solar system and creates different magnetic fields, with heliospheric current sheets.

Galaxy, oh beautiful galaxy,
how you twirl and twirl, round and round
come to me and dust off your Sun,
forget the supernovas and the red dwarfs,
milkyway is your name while the others were off.

The Milkyway Galaxy is about 90,000 light years far from one end to the other end. it is made up of stars, asteroids, meteoroids, comets and dark matter. This particular galaxy is 13.6 billion years old. Its center is believed to be made of star clusters and interstellar clouds, very close to Sagittarius. The galactic center and its white light and its celestial sphere are all visible from the earth. This barred spiral galaxy will collide with Andromeda galaxy in about a billion years from now together forming an elliptical galaxy with a new galactic core. This massive whirlpool of 300 billion stars is just one of billion of galaxies in the known universe.

Now on to the earth, the earth was a big rock made out of pure lava and carbon in its solid state. It was a star that has accidently collided with the first shuttle. The heat generated from the collision has been burning the core of the planet. It was just another star with no gravity, no magnetic fields, no rotation, and no future. It did not orbit around the Sun, and it was just sitting there, waiting to be discovered. Its numb state of life had nullified the existence of any animals or vegetations. There was no gas or dust gathering around its outer surface. It was just a big gigantic piece of rock of a star, without the reflections of the known Sun.

The first shuttle was a perfect pyramid of metal put together with laser like precision. The closest element on earth to this shuttle's outer and inner material is pure Mangenese (Mn) with atomic number 25 on the table of elements known to man. Its four nuclear engines are located at the tips of the pyramid and they all lead to the center core of the great ship, and they are connected to each other. So if there's powerful emission in one engine, the other ones balance each other's act. Its speed is in billions of light years at a time, that is why it can fly and glide from one galaxy to another galaxy in a matter of days. It also has laser guided hydrogen blasters, powerful enough to destroy the Sun into little tiny specs and fragments of what it is used to be.

The first shuttle was huge and enormous. I mean it was miles and miles long on each of its triangular side shape. It is as big as a diagnol line thru France and Germany put together to be exact. And that is just one side of the ship. It is definitely gigantic, as far as spaceships are concerned. The ship is so tough that it glides thru the mine fields of asteroids with such ease. It can destroy different commets with its laser sharp blasters.

The ship can manuver around any planet with its halogramic portals, which wrap themselves around any planet and gather perfectly in synch on the other side of the planet just as if it were never there. And then there is its speed: it is lightening fast, faster than lightyears at a time.

How can something so big, move so fast and accurate as it has? Its lightening speed of laser rays of photonic movement and waves of warp speed make the ship invisible to the ordinary eyes. The shuttle can move like a humming bird does thru the air, and in its triangular prism rotating on its core and center of gravity can move hundreds, thousands, millions and millions of lightyears at a split second. Now, the cargo of the ship is top secret, very vital to us all and it is for your eyes only, on need to know basis. The shuttle was carrying a cargo of top secret material; it is actually vital form of life on the blue planet: it is called H2O or as we humans call it on earth, plain water. It is so vital to us that seventy five percent of our body is made of water and two thirds of the earth is covered by it. This particular cargo, in its concentrated form was carried past the firey ring of the blue planet, past the Sun into the outer darkness past all the stars of the Milkyway Galaxy and almost into the belly of the black hole itself and collided with the known earth's body.

It was in the late hours of the second day of the flight, when the shuttle was approaching the burning Sun. Everything was going according to plan, which was to travel past the blue planet's outer ring and past the Sun and past the outskirts of the Milkyway Galaxy and right into the center of another black hole located exactly the opposite of the blue planet's black hole in a straight line; and the captain was suppose to unload the cargo there. And the distance to be traveled was about a million light years each way. The shuttle could have traveled this distance in about three days and three nights. That is about 72 hours which equals 4320 minutes away.

The ship's nuclear engines were fuming on track on the second day of the flight. The shining Sun was getting closer and closer. The captain put in motion the halogram phase. And after he commanded the shuttle to halogram itself around the Sun, the ship was disected by its internal laser portals, which separated the ship practically in half. With the laser light, the center of gravity of the pyramid was cut into two halfs. After a few minutes the millions and millions of halograms wrap around the Sun and gather themselves on the other side of the Sun. the shuttle was instantly put back together.

The captain was 100 percent healthy and okay, the cargo was in place, and the nuclear engines did not fail; and the ship itself uncloaked and appeared to be working just fine. All of the sudden, the shuttle could not change directions, and the captain tried to adjust the flight plan manually but it had no effect. The ship was headed towards earth head on. The captain then took no chances and put out the stress call, "save our soul", "save our soul", but there was no answer from the blue planet.

It took one second 00:00:01 for the captain to realize that this great ship of his was never getting off the earth. The collision was so big and loud that it sent shock waves thru the universe. The impact was so great that the pyramid's nose of the shuttle reached the core of the planet. It cut and cracked the surface and continued to descend down to the center of the earth. The ship is so fast that when it collided with earth it has peneterated the earth's surface thousands and thousands of feet below the ocean. it was what you can call an instantaneous polarization.

First the magnetic fields of the great ship took over the north and south poles; and all the ship electricity and power failed to exist. And then the earth started to rotate on its cylindrical axis. It also set the planet in an orbit around the sun. The gravity of the Sun and the rotation of the earth became constant and the moon was attracted to the earth. The ripples and ripples of the big banged collision was sent out throughout the universe at all angles. It was as if someone had thrown a piece of rock into the water. But it was the other way around, a drop of water had hit a piece of rock. The captain had no choice but to release the cargo into the rock.

The captain spent forty years in the belly of the ship, banging and hacking away at the nuclear engines of the shuttle. He must restart his engines, and it was no use, the power had left the ship and the cargo was all but empty. The captain had shut down all the nuclear engines and logged off the salvaged ship and dove into his emergency cacoon and at a press of the eject button, he surfaced in the Mediterranean sea at today's Jerusalem in Israel. The ship was buried deep, deep under the English Channel, under Germany, and France.

The collision was so hard that this water spattered all over the earth and buried the shuttle deep in the ground; and at a break of dawn, half of the known animals that today's man has identified flew up into the air and half of the animals were drowned in the water. It also rained and rained for forty years and forty times again and again, before the sky above the earth settled down. It took a very long time for the flood of dinosaurs and the carbonized, organic vegetations to be formed from the water and the earth's dust. The clouds finally settled down and a new day was upon the earth, at the crack of dawn.

Now, let me tell you about the captain of this great ship, captain Zero. He is the wisest human in the universe. He knows everything and anything to do with the Milkyway Galaxy. The blue planet is his home. He rarely makes a mistake and if he does make a mistake, he does not make the same mistake twice. He lives on trial and error. Captain Zero and all the animals of the earth and the cargo of this ship; these three elements of earth, the human and animal and water have coexisted for millions and millions of years. Now, after the great crash of the shuttle and earth, the captain had to abandoned ship and find himself in the midst of the earth's surface, where he had been walking on the actual ground for days and days. Then he heard the noise or saw an odd number that made him hate this world and it split him in two. He knew after that, that he is not alone on this mission of carrying this secret cargo. It was as if someone or something had stabbed him in the back of his body, and send chills up his spine.

Murderous, torturous, barbaric act of this white ghostly human; murder me, murder me how I wish it was me whom he had killed. He shed the first blood of a human on this forbidden place we call earth. This bloody dust of a rock took the first drop with such thirst that it has not yet been quenched after thousands and millions of years. And there it was, the missing link of today's people; it was clear as a Sun shining day that the cloaked unknown man had a number or said something to the captain that it killed the old man.

All I know now is that he died and went straight up to the sky about 2.32x 10 to the 56th power meters. I mean that he just blew up and exploded into the blue sky. In which direction did he go? Well if you can imagine a perfect straight line with laser precision from the very spot where the old man died, which is today's Jerusalem in Israel, shooting up into the atmosphere and goes past the outer darkness right thru the shining Sun and keeps going on through the Milkyway Galaxy and it keeps going to the center of the blue planet and right thru the center of the black hole that is if you can align these four points of direction: the earth, the Sun, the Milkyway Galaxy and the center of the black hole, that is where the blue planet is located and that is how far the old man traveled 2.32×10 to the 56th power meters and that is the direction.

But I can tell you this much that when the old man died, there came out five people out of him: one white man, one black man, one yellow man, one blue man and one red man. And they all went to different directions and settled down on earth's five different continents.

The original five individual human beings have different characteristics, the white man turns clear when he is mad and the black one turns darker black when he is upset and the yellow one turns orange when he is angry, the blue one turns into navy blue when he is mad and the red one turns purple when he is furious.

So the old man is captain Zero who showed no emotion as he left the abandoned ship behind. It was him who had become mute because of the fact of trying for forty years to get the ship restarted, or maybe it was the idea of losing all of his cargo and missing its target. In any case, his cacoon had bubbled up from the sea, and washed up ashore in Jerusalem, Israel.

The earth was full of water and animals and vegetation and gases and rocks. And captain Zero was walking among the dinosaurs of all sizes, when he checked his ears to find out if he can hear anything. But he was deaf and could not hear anything; no matter if it was a T-Rex or a small ant making the noise, the captain did not know the right frequency of the earth's different noises. So he started to walk up the beach and into the mountains and deserts.

It was on top of an hill where he had been walking and looking for any clue on how and what went wrong. But he could only hear his heart beat when he saw the odd number appear or he heard the other human's noise. The captain's heart started to speed up and break in half simultaneously. And then he flew up into the sky. First he passed Mars and then Saturn in his flight suit made out of Mangenese (Mn) material. Then he passed around the Sun and the Milkyway Galaxy and past the ring of fire with the last drop of water he had with him; and then the captain landed on the blue planet.

He restarted everything he had and jumped into a smaller fighting shuttle, and came back to earth in three days. He has landed the shuttle on the Bermuda Islands in the Atlantic Ocean. And this time, he brought with him five blue soldiers in this fighter ship and two women from a different planet.

The old man has brought five soldiers to guard the five different colored people. And these blue soldiers have similar characteristics and shapes and minds and have come from the outer space in order to protect and help these different colored humans.

Now today's modern man is the evolution of thousands of generations of multiplying himself into these different colors. And with global warming and nuclear waste and other problems of this world, the earth is heading towards its final days where it will either get depolorized and break in half after all the lava and the dirt and rocks have consumed all the earth's water supply, every last drop of it. Or all the earth's atmosphere will turn into nitrogen and then turn earth into a cold solid and liquid Nitrogen star with nothing left to survive on. The earth as we know it, will be Nitrogenized.

As me and the old man sat on a bench watching the sunset, the old man said to me that there is only enough room for twelve people for the final journey back home for the two women and the ten men. "So, how will you go back home captain?", I asked the old man. "Why do you ask young one?" he responded. Because it is so hard to say good-bye to the ones you love, I said to him. "How would you know to love something that you have never seen or heard before?" he said. So, I told him the following story:

It was a beautiful day in the Fall season and without any reason at all, I just kept staring into the water. The pool was full of leaves, some were dry on one side, some had wet spots on them, and others were emerging just below the surface. What was I looking for I can not remember. The air was cold and chilling; even though there was crisp slight wind in the air, you could not feel it. I began to see my image in the pool as I leaned forward carefully, the water had turned black because nobody was taking care of it. I started to walk towards the gardener's house. As I walked gingerly on top of the leaves, there was a gust of wind down the small garden leading into the garden house. As the bed of roses were shaking, I began to wonder where he was. I got closer and closer, and crushed more leaves on my way to the garden house, I tapped on the blurry glass door but there was no answer. I was thinking to myself that I had come to say good-bye and he is not there. But how can this be, he said I can "come back anytime that I wanted", oh well if he is not home, he is not home. I just didn't want him to say that "the lights are on and nobody is home"; plus am I just a number among 6 billion people on earth or this old man has some kind of faith in me? so I just left and started to walk down the wide, steep street, forever.

THE END

Printed in the United States
By Bookmasters